This book belongs to:

....

To Linda, without whom a very small part of
this book would not have been possible! K.G.

In loving memory of Joan and Ian J.F.

First published in hardback in 2014 by Hodder Children's Books
First published in paperback in 2015

Text copyright © Kes Gray 2014
Illustration copyright © Jim Field 2014

Hodder Children's Books
338 Euston Road, London NW1 3BH

Hodder Children's Books Australia
Level 17/207 Kent Street, Sydney, NSW 2000

A catalogue record of this book is available from the British Library.

ISBN: 978 1 444 91086 5
10 9 8 7 6 5 4 3 2

Printed in Spain

Hodder Children's Books is a division of Hachette Children's Books.

An Hachette UK Company

www.hachette.co.uk

www.kesgray.com www.jimfield.co.uk

Oi FROG!

Kes Gray
and **Jim Field**

h
Hodder
Children's
Books

A division of Hachette Children's Books

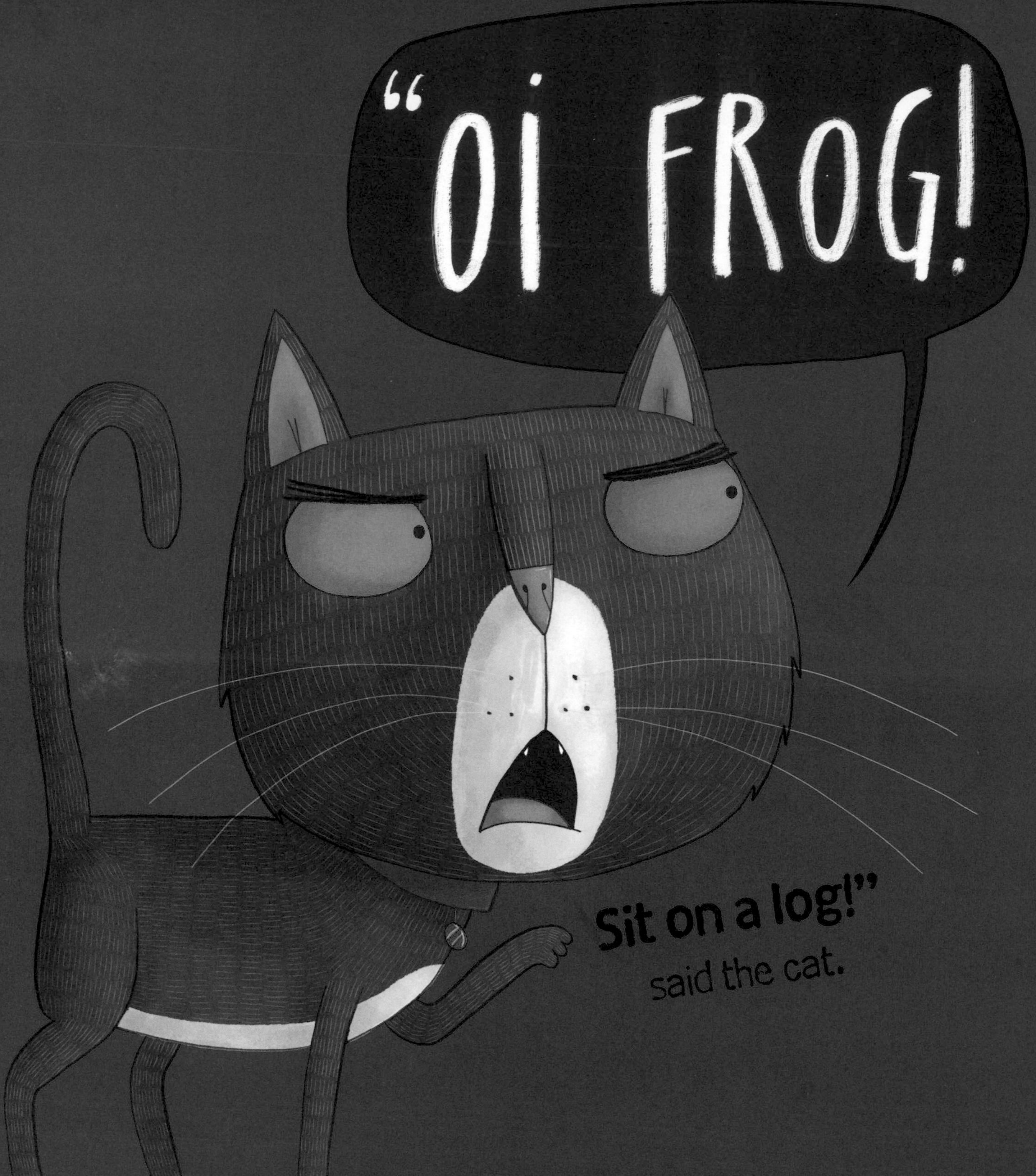

Sit on a log!”
said the cat.

"But I don't want to **sit** on a **log**," said the frog.
"Logs are all nobbly and uncomfortable.
And they can give you splinters in your bottom."

"I don't care," said the cat.
"You're a **frog**, so you must sit on a **log**."

"Can't I sit on a **mat?**"
asked the frog.

"**Only** cats sit on **mats**," said the cat.

"What about a **chair?**"
said the frog.
"I wouldn't mind sitting
on a chair."

"Hares sit on **chairs,"**
said the cat.

"Perhaps I could sit on a **stool?**" said the frog.

"**Mules** sit on **stools**,"
said the cat.

"What about a **sofa?**" said the frog.

"I could **stretch right out** on a sofa!"

"**Gophers** sit on **sofas**," said the cat.

"It's very simple really.

"What do **lions** sit on?"
asked the frog.

"Lions sit on **irons,"**
said the cat.

"**Ouch!**" said the frog.
"What do **parrots** sit on?"

"**Parrots** sit on **carrots**,"
said the cat.

"**Lions**
sit on
irons
and
parrots
sit on
carrots."

"Doesn't sound very comfortable," said the frog.

"It's not about being comfortable," said the cat.
"It's about doing the **right thing.**"

"What do **foxes** sit on?" asked the frog.

"**Foxes** sit on **boxes**," said the cat.

"**Foxes** sit on **boxes** and **fleas** sit on peas."

"What do **goats** sit on?" asked the frog.

"**Goats** sit on **coats**,"
said the cat.

"**Goats** sit on **coats**,
cows sit on **ploughs** and
storks sit on **forks**."

"What do **gorillas** sit on?"
asked the frog.

"Gorillas
sit on
pillars,"
said the cat.

"Gorillas sit on **pillars,**

"What do **seals** sit on?" asked the frog.

"Don't you know **anything?**"
said the cat.

"**Seals** sit on
wheels,

doves sit on gloves,
newts sit on flutes,
lizards sit on wizards and
apes sit on grapes."

"What about **puffins?**" asked the frog.

"**Puffins** sit on **muffins**," said the cat.

"Puffins sit on muffins,
snakes sit on cakes,
owls sit on towels,
gibbons sit on ribbons,
lambs sit on jams,
bees sit on keys, and
pumas sit on satsumas."

"Well I **never** knew that," said the frog.

"Well you do now," said the cat.

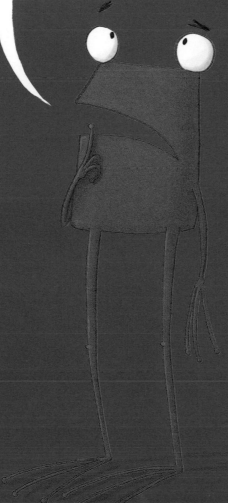

"**WHAT DO DOGS SIT ON?**"

asked the frog.

"I was hoping you weren't going to ask that," said the cat...

978 1 444 90015 6

Leave Me Alone
A tale of what happens when you face up to a bully

978 0 340 95711 0

Kes Gray

MUM AND DAD GLUE

Illustrated by Lee Wildish

978 1 444 90016 3

WORRIES GO AWAY!

KES GRAY AND LEE WILDISH

More fabulous books written by Kes Gray

978 1 444 92141 0

A must-have for working mums everywhere. — Rachel, a mum

Mummy Goes to Work
Written by Kes Gray
Illustrated by David Milgrim

PEDRO has a Bump!
Kes Gray & Mary McQuillan
With over 50 stickers!

978 1 444 90023 1

Baby on Board
Kes Gray
Sarah Nayler

978 1 444 92090 1